by **Lauren Thompson**
pictures by **Derek Anderson**

Simon & Schuster Books for Young Readers
NEW YORK LONDON TORONTO SYDNEY SINGAPORE

Mama Duck had five little ducklings, Widdle, Waddle, Piddle, Puddle, and Little Quack.

One day Mama said, "Let's play hide-and-seek. You hide, and I'll try to find you."

COUNT ALONG WITH THE
QUACK-U-LATOR!
= 5

"You won't find *me*!" cried Widdle.
"You'll never find *me*!" cried Waddle.
"Just try and find *me*!" cried Piddle.
"You'll find me *last*!" cried Puddle.
And Little Quack cried, "I'll find the *BEST* hiding place of all!"

Mama covered her eyes. She began to count, "One . . . two . . ."
Widdle found a dark place to hide.

FOUR DUCKLINGS

− = 3

Mama counted, “Three . . . four . . .”
Waddle found a wet place to hide.

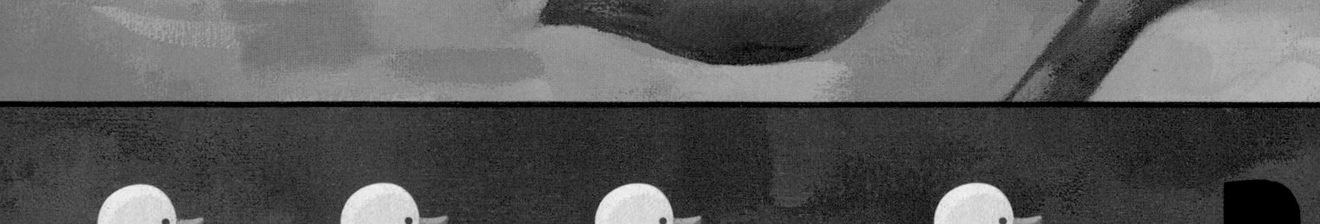
- = 2

Mama counted, "Five . . . six . . ."
Piddle found a high place to hide.

Mama Duck counted, “Seven . . . eight . . .”
Puddle found a leafy place to hide.

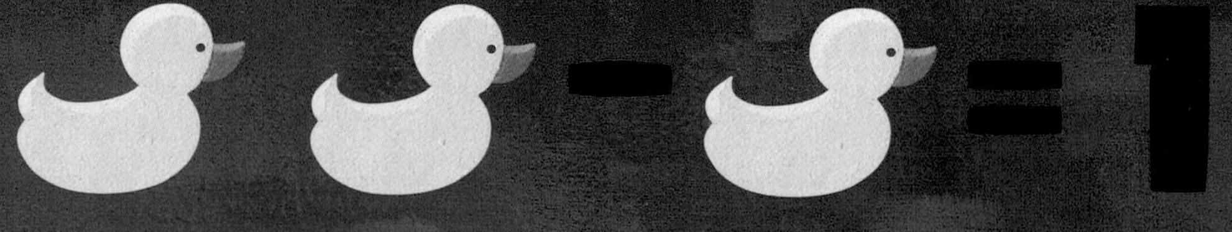

ONE DUCKLING

Mama counted, "Nine . . ."
Oh, no! Where should Little Quack hide?

Mama called out, “Ten! Here I come!”
Little Quack found a *quick* place to hide
—right behind Mama!

Mama paddled over to a log.
"Any ducklings down there?" she called.
"Here I am!" cried Widdle.
"That's one little duckling found," said Mama.
"Who will I find next?"

Mama paddled over to the lilies.
"Any ducklings under here?" she called.
"You found me!" cried Waddle.
"That's two little ducklings found," said Mama.
"Who will I find next?"

Mama paddled over to a branch.
"Any ducklings up there?" she called.
"It's me!" cried Piddle.
"That's three little ducklings found," said Mama.
"Who will I find next?"

Mama paddled over to the reeds.
"Any ducklings here?" she called.
"I'm here!" called Puddle.
"That's four little ducklings found," said Mama. "Now, where is Little Quack?"

Mama paddled over to the shore.
"Little Quack, are you hiding here?" she called.
No, Little Quack wasn't hiding on the shore.

Mama paddled over to a rock.
“Little Quack, are you are hiding here?” she called.
No, Little Quack wasn’t hiding near the rock.

Then Mama Duck called out,
"Little Quack, where *are* you?"

"Here I am!" cried Little Quack. "Right behind you, Mama!"
"There you are!" said Mama. "You *did* find the best hiding place of all!"

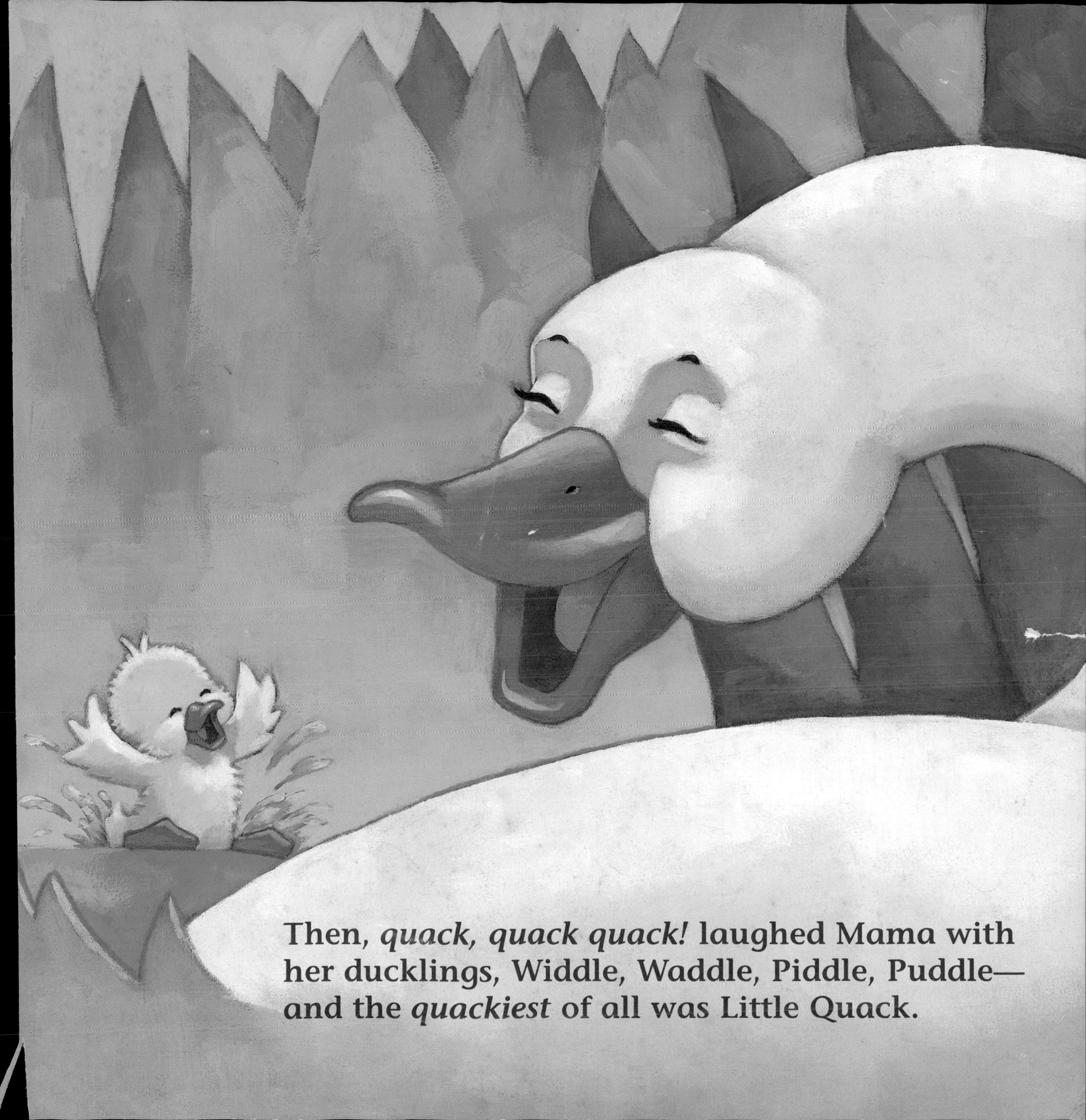

Then, *quack, quack quack!* laughed Mama with her ducklings, Widdle, Waddle, Piddle, Puddle— and the *quackiest* of all was Little Quack.

To Owen, our "quacky"
little duckling
—L. T.

For Mom and Dad
—D. A.

SIMON & SCHUSTER BOOKS FOR YOUNG READERS
An imprint of Simon & Schuster Children's Publishing Division
1230 Avenue of the Americas, New York, New York 10020

Book design by Greg Stadnyk
The text for this book is set in Stone Informal and 99.
The illustrations for this book are rendered in acrylic on canvas.
Manufactured in Mexico
2 4 6 8 10 9 7 5 3 1
CIP data for this book is available from the Library of Congress.
ISBN 0-689-85722-5